This book belongs to:

....

....

Naughty Nestor

Created by small world creations ltd

igloo

Nestor's Mum was going to visit Daisy Cat next door. "I'll be gone all morning," she said, "so I've asked Old Tom to come and keep an eye on you." She kissed Nestor and went out.

Nestor did not want a babysitter. When Old Tom arrived, Nestor hid until he went away again.

"Now I can do exactly what I want!" said Naughty Nestor, heading for his water bowl.

First he gobbled all the food in his bowl. Then he gobbled all of Mum's food as well. Then he jumped into his water-bowl with all four feet – splosh!
The water went everywhere.

Nestor rolled and kicked and paddled in his water-bowl. He wet his tummy and his tail and even his whiskers.

He played until every drop of water was on the kitchen floor and his water-bowl was empty.

"Brrr!" said Nestor. "I need to get warm." He spied the living-room curtains. They were thick and red and velvety. Nestor climbed into them and rubbed himself up and down. "Perfect," he purred, as he began to warm up.

The curtains made an excellent slide. They made an excellent swing, as well.

After a while, Nestor climbed right up to the curtain pole, crawled across it and took a flying leap on to...

...the chandelier in the middle of the room. "Wow!" thought Nestor, looking down on the living room. "I'm like a bird in a tree!"

He started to swing the chandelier, rocking it backwards and forwards until the little pieces of glass clinked together.

"I'm flying!" cried Nestor. Then he lost his balance, shot off the chandelier, flipped over in the air and landed safely...

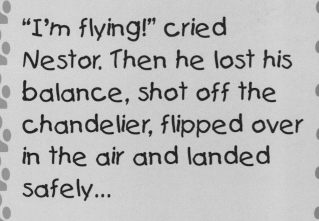

...in the middle of the sofa.

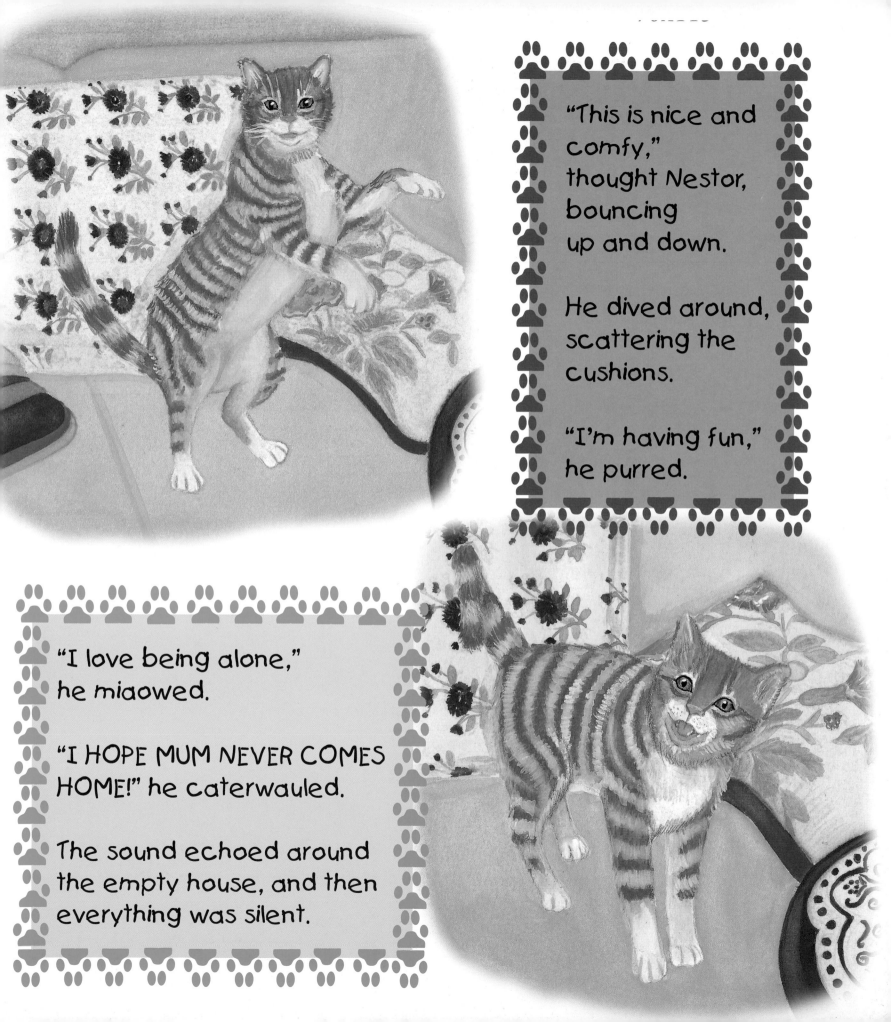

"This is nice and comfy," thought Nestor, bouncing up and down.

He dived around, scattering the cushions.

"I'm having fun," he purred.

"I love being alone," he miaowed.

"I HOPE MUM NEVER COMES HOME!" he caterwauled.

The sound echoed around the empty house, and then everything was silent.

"I wonder when Mum IS coming home," thought Nestor suddenly.

He jumped down from the sofa and padded back into the kitchen.

"I'm thirsty," he thought, but his water-bowl was empty.

"And I'm hungry," he thought, but he had eaten all the food.

Nestor didn't feel like being naughty any more. He felt sad and lonely.

Just then, Old Tom put his head through the cat flap.

"There you are, Nestor," he said. "I thought I'd find you here, sooner or later."

"I want my Mum," said Nestor.

"I'm sure she won't be much longer," said Tom kindly.

He tiptoed onto the wet kitchen floor.

"Has there been a hurricane in here?" he asked.

Suddenly Nestor saw what Tom saw. He saw the kitchen floor covered in water and all the feeding bowls standing on their heads.

In the living room he saw that the curtains were damp and out of place, the sofa was all messed up and the chandelier was still swinging gently from side to side.

"Oh dear," said Nestor, blinking very fast.

"You have been enjoying yourself," chuckled Old Tom.

"The secret to making a great big mess," said Tom, turning over the feeding bowls with his nose, "is to tidy it up again afterwards."

He pushed the dishes to the side.

Then he showed Nestor how to lick up the spilled water on the floor.

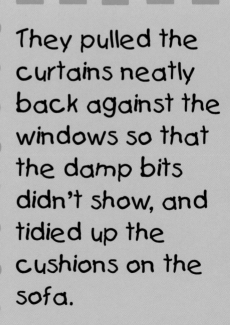

They pulled the curtains neatly back against the windows so that the damp bits didn't show, and tidied up the cushions on the sofa.

Nestor just had time to jump down from the sofa and lick his fur into place before Mum came in through the cat-flap.

"What a good kitten you are, Nestor," said Mum, looking around at the tidy house. "You deserve a treat. How about a nice mouse-hunt after dark?"

"Yes please, Mum!" cried Nestor. "And next time you go out, can Old Tom come and babysit again?" Old Tom chuckled and gave Naughty Nestor a big, secret wink.

The end.